7×7 Tales
of a
Sevensleeper

7×7 Tales
of a
Sevensleeper

by Hanna Johansen

illustrated by Käthi Bhend

faber and faber
LONDON · BOSTON

First published in Switzerland in 1985
by Verlag Nagel and Kimche AG, Zurich
as *Siebenschläfergeschichten*

This English translation first published
in the United States of America in 1989
by E. P. Dutton, a division of Penguin Books USA Inc.

This edition first published in Great Britain in 1990
by Faber and Faber Limited
3 Queen Square London WC1N 3AU
This paperback edition first published in 1992

Printed in England by Clays Ltd, St Ives plc

© 1985 Verlag Nagel and Kimche AG, Zurich
Illustrations © Kathi Bhend, 1985
Translation © Christopher Franceschelli, 1989

A CIP record for this book is available
from the British Library

ISBN 0-571-16506-0

2 4 6 8 10 9 7 5 3 1

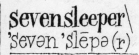

sevensleeper
'sevən 'slēpə (r)

<u>n</u>: a fat dormouse,
<u>or</u> hazel mouse, a small
squirrel-like rodent.
Sevensleepers live
in trees and feed
on acorns
and nuts
(especially hazelnuts);

they sleep deeply
during the day
and for almost
seven months
during the winter.

"I am
a sevensleeper.
In the autumn,
when it gets too cold for
sevensleepers, they stuff
themselves with food,
look for a cave,
curl up with their tails
over their heads,
cover their ears,
and close their eyes.
Then they sleep for seven months.

"Good morning,"
said the Sevensleeper.
He had just
woken up from his winter sleep.
"Just in time," said his mother.
It really was just in time,
because Easter had come and gone
and the holidays were over.
"Do you like sevensleepers?"
said the Sevensleeper.

6 ·

"I don't know," answered his mother.
"But you must know,"
said the Sevensleeper.
"Either you like them
or you don't.
Anyway, everyone likes them."
"Well, I've never seen one,"
said his mother.
"Me neither. They hide
but that doesn't matter."

Then the Sevensleeper said,
"Sevensleepers
are my favorite animals."
"What do they look like?"
"Soft and cuddly,"
said the Sevensleeper.

"Then I like them," said his mother.
"If we are very careful,
maybe we'll find one."
"Maybe," said the Sevensleeper.
"You just have to look out for
the nutshells they leave behind."
"That sounds easy enough,"
said his mother.
"It is.
They eat quite a lot of nuts."

"Oh," said his mother.
Just once she would have liked
to have seen a sevensleeper.
"You can keep them in a cage,"
said the Sevensleeper.
"Then we'd have to be very careful
that they didn't gnaw their way out."
Then he said, "Until we have one,
I'll be your sevensleeper.
And you can pretend
he looks just like me."

Once upon a time
there was a sevensleeper
and it was his birthday.
He was seven years old.
Early that morning
he sat on
the edge of his bed and said,
"This is the most important day
of my life."

On the table
was a birthday cake.
And on the cake
burned seven candles.
Seven is much better than six,
thought the Sevensleeper.
Then he unwrapped his presents:
a packet of marzipan vegetables,
a seven-cornered flannel,
a toy steam shovel,
a diary with a little golden key,
and a pencil that wrote
in four colours.

And finally a big box
of roller skates.
The Sevensleeper was very happy.
Then one of his sevensleeper ears
sadly drooped.
"What's the matter?" asked his parents.
"Nothing," said the Sevensleeper.
"Is something missing?" asked his parents.
"Hmmm," said the Sevensleeper.
"I know what's missing,"
said his little brother
and pulled a tiny package
out of his trouser pocket.
"That's my present," he said.
My little brother isn't half as dumb
as I thought,
thought the Sevensleeper.
Now he had seven presents.
There was a rubber eraser
that smelled like chocolate.
"Thank you," said the Sevensleeper.
"Will it erase my four-colour pencil?"

"Of course," said his brother,
but the Sevensleeper
didn't believe him.

That night the Sevensleeper wrote
the first sentence in his new diary
in green pencil:

Now I am SEVEN.

Then he turned out the light.
But he couldn't sleep.
I must write it another way,
thought the Sevensleeper.
It must be in red.
He turned the light on again,
picked up his diary,
and started to erase
with his new eraser.
"I knew it wouldn't work,"
said the Sevensleeper.
Then he wrote the second sentence
in red:

This is the most IMPORTANT day of my life!

The most important
thing about a
sevensleeper
is the number 7.
That's why every
evening you have to tell him
a sevensleeper story—
or seven other stories.
That works too.
Sevensleepers can
count exactly to seven.
They stop after that.
They'd rather start at the beginning again.

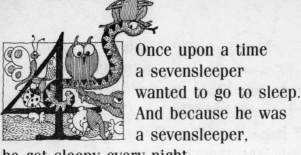

Once upon a time
a sevensleeper
wanted to go to sleep.
And because he was
a sevensleeper,
he got sleepy every night
at seven o'clock.
He curled up between
his seven stuffed toys.
"I can't sleep,"
said the Sevensleeper.
"What's the matter?" asked his mother.
"It's seven o'clock, and you're sleepy."
"First I have to say good night to my
seven stuffed toys."
And he said good night to his
seven stuffed toys:
the owl, the snake, the frog,
the butterfly, the clown,
the fish, the ladybug,
and finally the crocodile.
"I can't sleep,"
said the Sevensleeper.

"What's the matter?" asked his mother.
"It's seven o'clock, you're sleepy,
and you've said good night to
your seven stuffed toys."
"I know," said the Sevensleeper,
"but something's wrong.
I have to count my toys."
Then the Sevensleeper
counted his seven toys:
the owl, the snake, the frog,
the butterfly, the clown,
the fish, the ladybug,
and finally the crocodile.
"You see," he said.
"There aren't seven.
There are eight."
"But that doesn't matter,"
said his mother.
"Yes it does," said the Sevensleeper.
"A sevensleeper needs
seven animals, not eight.
I'll have to put one away,"
said the Sevensleeper.

"Eeny, meeny, miney moe . . ."
The Sevensleeper had to count
seven times to figure out
which of the toys to put away.
It was the crocodile.
But the crocodile was unhappy
and started to cry.
"You don't love me anymore,"
he sobbed.
"Of course I do," said the Sevensleeper.
"I love you very much.
But if you are
a real crocodile
you'll manage to
lie in front of the bed
tonight and protect us."
"All right," said the crocodile.
"But tomorrow
it's someone else's turn."
The Sevensleeper
curled up
with his seven animals.
"I can't fall asleep," he said.

"What's the matter?" asked his mother.
"It's seven o'clock,
you have your seven animals,
and you're tired."
"Yes," said the Sevensleeper.
"But there's something wrong.
Let me see your watch.
You see," he said.
"It's not seven anymore.
It's already eight o'clock."
"That doesn't matter,"
said his mother worriedly.
"You can go to sleep at eight."
"No," said the Sevensleeper.
"A sevensleeper goes to bed at seven,
not at eight."
"That's terrible,"
said his mother.
"I can't stand it."
But the Sevensleeper said,
"That doesn't matter. I'll just wait
until it's seven o'clock again."

Once upon a time
there was a sevensleeper
who went out into the woods.
Because
every sevensleeper
just has to climb.
And if there aren't any woods,
a garden will do.
And if there's no garden,
a few trees
will do for a start.
Some trees stood
right in front of the house
where the Sevensleeper lived.
They were good enough
to practise on.
Their tops were especially good.
They have branches
a sevensleeper can run around on,
thought the Sevensleeper.
Fortunately there was also a
little tree.

More a bush than a tree.
That's where the Sevensleeper
practised climbing.
"What are you doing up there?"
asked his little brother.
"Looking for food,"
said the Sevensleeper.
"You're crazy," said his brother.
"You're crazy,"
said the Sevensleeper.
"What sort of food?"
asked his brother.
"Nuts," said the Sevensleeper.
"Throw one down,"
said his brother.
"No," said the Sevensleeper.
"You're not getting any."
"Why not?" asked his brother.
"Because it isn't even a nut tree,"
said the Sevensleeper.

 Once upon a time
a sevensleeper
sat down to lunch.
First he took some potatoes.
One.
Two.
Three.
Four.
Five.
Six.
Seven.
"Isn't that an awful lot?"
asked his father.
"No," said the Sevensleeper,
"I have to have seven."
Then he took some peas. Seven peas.
"Don't you want more than that?"
asked his mother.
"No," he said.
"I have to have seven."
Then he took some fish sticks.
One. Two. Three. Four. Five. Six. Seven.

"Hey," said his brother.
"Leave some for me."
"You're only four,"
said the Sevensleeper.
"You don't need that many."
The Sevensleeper couldn't eat
his seven potatoes.
"You said yourself
there had to be seven,"
said his father.
The Sevensleeper began to wish
he weren't a sevensleeper anymore.
The Sevensleeper couldn't eat his
seven fish sticks either.
Now and then he cut off a little bit
and dipped it into the ketchup,
but it still had to be eaten.
"You can give it to me,"
said his brother.
"Just this once,"
said the Sevensleeper.
"But don't think
it'll make you grow.

But what I'd really like
is some more peas,"
said the Sevensleeper.
His mother looked into the dish
and said,
"You're in luck.
There are only seven left."

The seventh
sevensleeper story
is a special story.
It is a secret
that must not be given away.
If you can find out what it is, you can
write it down.....

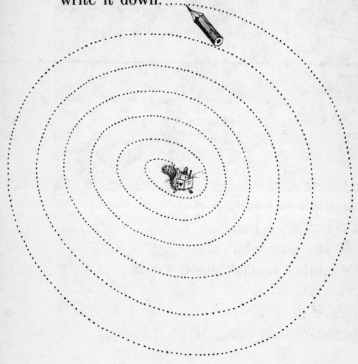

22 ·

Once upon a time
there was a sevensleeper
who slunk into
the bathroom
to wash.
It took him seven minutes
and seven drops of water.
"Did you get washed?"
his mother asked
when he returned to the kitchen.
He nodded.
"It doesn't look like it,"
said his mother.
Then she said, "And did you
brush your teeth?"
The Sevensleeper shook his head.
"Why not?" she asked.
"I couldn't,"
said the Sevensleeper sadly.
"Maybe you're still too tired,"
said his mother.
"No," said the Sevensleeper.
"The problem is the toothbrush.

I can't brush my teeth
with that toothbrush."
"Why not?" his mother asked.
"It's brand new."
"It has eight bristles,"
the Sevensleeper said crossly.
"Oh no, not again,"
said his mother
and dropped into her chair.
"It's not that bad,"
said the Sevensleeper.
"I know just what to do."
He went to the bathroom,
got a pair of nail clippers,
cut off one of the eight bristles,
squeezed some toothpaste onto his new
seven-bristled toothbrush,
and brushed his teeth.

"It's high time,"
said his mother,
"you put away
your seven toys."
When he heard that
the Sevensleeper sat
down on the floor.
"Seven toys here," he said,
"and seven toys there.
Seven toys here.
And seven toys there."
Then he sighed, "I've been
cleaning up for seven hours."
"No," said his mother,
"seven minutes."
The Sevensleeper said,
"Then it's high time I stopped."

26 ·

Once upon a time
there was a sevensleeper
who loved to go to town
with his mother.
Every time
they waited for the bus
in front of the train station
he grew tremendously hungry.
It wasn't the train station's fault.
"I'm so hungry," he would say.
"We'll be home soon,"
said his mother.

"I can't wait that long,"
said the Sevensleeper.
"Should we buy you a sandwich?"
asked his mother.
"I'd much rather have french fries,"
said the Sevensleeper.

There just happened to be
a street vendor who sold french fries
right behind them.
"Seven french fries, please,"
said the Sevensleeper.
"I don't think they count them,"
said his mother.
"You'll have to take a whole bag."
"Seven bags, please,"
said the Sevensleeper.

 Once upon a time
there was
a sevensleeper
who couldn't run
as fast as the others.
That made him cross.
Whenever he and his
seven friends got together
and had a race
he never won.
But the Sevensleeper
loved to race.
"What we need," he said,
"are new rules."
So they started
playing by
the new rule that

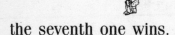

the seventh one wins.

A sevensleeper
once woke up
in the middle
of the night.
"Why can't I sleep?"
said the Sevensleeper.
"It must be
a special night."
Everything was quiet.

The Sevensleeper went to the window
and looked out.
The sky was black and full of stars.
"Too bad they're so far away,"
said the Sevensleeper.
"When I grow up
I'm going to build
myself a telescope.
I'll become an astronomer
and will see everything that's there."
His mother woke up.
"Why aren't you asleep?"
she asked.

30 ·

"What are the stars called?"
the Sevensleeper replied.
"The seven up there
are the Big Dipper,"
his mother said.
But they didn't look like a dipper.
"They should be called Sevenstars,"
said the Sevensleeper.
Suddenly a star shot across the sky.
When that happens you can make a wish
but you can't tell anyone what it is.
And what did
the Sevensleeper wish for?
That none of the stars
in the Big Dipper
would ever fall down.

 Once upon a time
a sevensleeper
counted his money.
"One.
Two.
Three.
Four.
Five.
Six.
Seven."

He made a little pile
and then he counted
the coins for the next pile.
"One. Two. Three.
Four. Five.
Six. Seven."

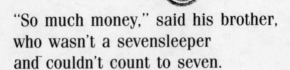

"So much money," said his brother,
who wasn't a sevensleeper
and couldn't count to seven.

"Yes," said the Sevensleeper,
and continued counting.
"What are you going to do with it all?"
"I'm saving up," said the Sevensleeper.
"Oh," said his brother.
"And when you have lots of money
you'll buy an airplane."
"No," said the Sevensleeper.
"Will you buy a car?"
asked his brother.
"No," said the Sevensleeper.
"What will you buy?"
"A seven-color pencil,"
said the Sevensleeper.
"Do they make those?"
asked his brother.
"Of course they do,"
said the Sevensleeper.

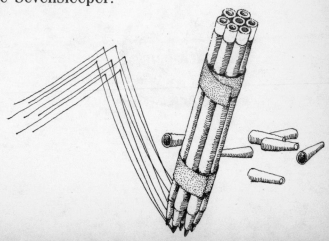

Once upon a time
there was
a sevensleeper
who had a big secret.
But the secret was so small
that he could hide it
in a nutshell.
No one ever discovered what it was,
except you.

 "What's a sevensleeper?"
asked his brother.
"It's someone,"
answered the Sevensleeper,
"who sleeps for seven months."
"How boring," said his brother.
"No it's not,"
said the Sevensleeper.
"Why not sleep when
everything else is so boring."
"I want to be a sevensleeper too,"
said his brother.
"No," said the Sevensleeper.
"You can't."
"Then I want to fly."
"You can be a sparrow,"
said the Sevensleeper.
"Are they big?" asked his brother.
"No, they're very small."

"Then I'll be an owl. They're big,"
said his brother.

"Then you'll have to sleep all day long,"
said the Sevensleeper.
"I don't care."
"And you can eat me up,"
said the Sevensleeper.
"I'm an owl," said his brother.
"You can be a squirrel,"
said the Sevensleeper.
"Owl. Owl. Owl."
It's bad for sevensleepers
to have owls for enemies
because they're so dangerous.
But the Sevensleeper had always liked owls.
They were almost as beautiful
as sevensleepers.
But ever since
his brother became an owl
and started hunting him,
he didn't like owls anymore.

Once upon a time
a sevensleeper
was cracking nuts.
"Give me some,"
said his brother.
"What kind of
an animal are you?"
asked the Sevensleeper.
"I'm an owl," said the brother.
"Owls don't eat nuts,"
said the Sevensleeper.
"Then I'm a squirrel," said the brother.
"If you're a squirrel you can have
as many nuts as you want.
But then
you can't try
to eat me anymore,"
said the Sevensleeper.
"OK," said his brother.
They didn't stop eating
until they had run out of nuts.
The table was littered with shells
so you knew

that sevensleepers had been there.
"Who ate all the nuts?"
his father asked.
"It must have been
the sevensleepers,"
said the Sevensleeper.
"Then they should have
cleaned up the shells," his father said.
"Sevensleepers never clean up,"
said the Sevensleeper.
"That's for the squirrel to do."

 A sevensleeper
lay in his tree hole
shivering.
A horrible face
loomed up in front of him.
A huge jaw with sharp teeth
opened wide, ready to eat him.
"Help!" the Sevensleeper cried.
"Help! Help! Help!"

Then the horrible face disappeared.
"Thank goodness," said the Sevensleeper,
"it was only a dream."

40 ·

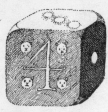 Once upon a time
there was a sevensleeper
who didn't want to play
Ludo anymore.
His brother had
already won three times.
The Sevensleeper
didn't mind losing
as long as his brother
didn't win.
"It's the dice's fault," he said.
"You always say that," said his brother.
"Because it's true,"
said the Sevensleeper.
"We could use some other dice,"
said his brother.
"That wouldn't help,"
said the Sevensleeper.
"They all only go up to six."
There was a time he didn't mind
dice having six sides,
but after he turned seven,
he stopped liking them.

"They're for little kids," he said.
"But that's how they have to be,"
said his mother.
"No," said the Sevensleeper.
"I'm going to invent my own dice.
Better ones.
And then you won't win anymore
and I'll get really rich
because I invented some new dice."
"Bet you can't,"
said his brother.
The Sevensleeper sat down
at the table
to invent a pair of dice
with seven sides.

He wasn't the first
to try.
But he just might be the first
to succeed.

 "Sevensleepers
are lucky,"
said the Sevensleeper.
"Everyone likes them."
"They taste good too,"
said his father.
"No," said the Sevensleeper.
"Didn't you know that people
used to fatten sevensleepers,
and fry them up and eat them?"
"That's terrible," said the Sevensleeper.
"That's a great idea," said his brother.
"They should . . ."
said the Sevensleeper.
"They should what?"
"They should fry owls,"
said the Sevensleeper.

 Almost all
sevensleepers
love to eat cake.
Only very rarely
there's one who
dislikes cake and
who would rather eat spinach,
fish, and frog legs.
You'd have to look
pretty hard to find one.
Many of the sevensleepers
who love cake also love to bake.
Many don't.
Maybe it's because
baking takes so long.
Maybe not.
A sevensleeper
who wanted to bake a cake
spread all the ingredients
out on the table.
"We don't have enough eggs," he said.
"How many do you need?"
asked his father.

"Three times seven," he said.
"I think that's too many,"
said his father.
"No," said the Sevensleeper,
"that's just right."
And when his father, who had also
baked a few cakes in his time,
didn't want to believe him,
the Sevensleeper added,
"You'll see."
He bought three times seven eggs,
and because
he wanted to bake a chocolate cake
he bought seven bars of chocolate.
Then he stirred the dough,
with seven hundred grams of butter,
seven hundred grams of sugar,
three times seven eggs,
seven hundred grams
of melted chocolate,
seven tablespoons of chopped nuts,
and seven hundred grams of flour
with seven tablespoons of baking powder.

It was hard work.
The Sevensleeper had to lick off
seven fingers full of dough right away.

With the rest he made seven cakes.
They'll be the best cakes in the world,
he thought.
"How long do they have to bake?"
His father considered the question
then he answered,
"Five times seven minutes."
"Too long," said the Sevensleeper.
"I'll never be able to wait that long."

 Once upon a time
a sevensleeper
took his
seven cakes
out of the oven
and put them
on the table.
"Who's going to eat them all?"
asked his mother.
"Me," said the Sevensleeper.
"But you can have a taste."
They smelled like
the best cakes in the whole world.
And they tasted that way.
But anyone who wants to know
how sevensleeper cakes
really taste
will just have to bake one.

7

"Who do you love most?
Me or my brother?"
"You."

"And what do you tell my brother
when he asks you that question?"
"Him."

"And which of us
are you lying to?"
"I never lie."

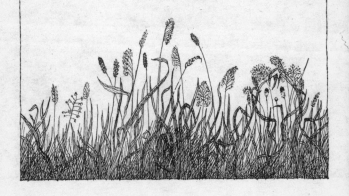

 Once upon a time
a sevensleeper
couldn't stand
the sight of cake
because he had eaten so many of them.
"Could I have a piece of
sevensleeper cake?"
his brother asked.
The Sevensleeper didn't answer.
"Could I please have a piece of cake?"
his brother repeated.
Still no answer.
"Why don't you say something?"
said his brother.
"Because
I don't understand
human speech,"
said the Sevensleeper.
"You have to
learn to speak
Sevensleeperese."
"How?" asked his brother.
The Sevensleeper didn't answer.

"You don't even know
how to speak it," said his brother.
"Of course I know how.
But I'll never tell you."
"Because you don't know how,"
said his brother.

"Oh all right," said the Sevensleeper.
"You can have
a piece of sevensleeper cake."

 "My seven friends are
going away on vacation,"
said the Sevensleeper.
"Where are we going?"
"We're staying here," said his mother.
"Too bad," said the Sevensleeper.
"Or maybe it's not so bad.
I'll just tell them
we sailed the seven seas."

3 Sevensleepers never know
when to stop eating.
The owl said,
"Sevensleepers
shouldn't eat so much pudding."
"Sevensleepers eat everything,"
said the Sevensleeper.
"You're lying," said the owl.
"They don't eat fish."
"Of course not,"
said the Sevensleeper.
"But they eat insects and snails."
"What are insects?" asked the owl.
"Bugs and beetles and spiders,"
said the Sevensleeper.
"Yucko!" said the owl.
"They really like them?"
That evening the Sevensleeper
received a beautifully wrapped package
from his brother.
"It's a present for you,"
he said. "Something to eat."
"Thank you," said the Sevensleeper.

But that was before he had opened
the present.

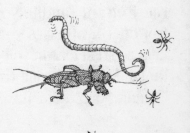

Once upon a time
a sevensleeper
had a brother.
Other people
had brothers too,
but the Sevensleeper
had a problem
other people didn't.
He had the bad luck
of having a horrible brother.
A really unbearable one.
And he was much too small.
He'd been too small right from the start,
but recently things had gotten worse.
There really wasn't anything useful
to do with him.
"Dad," said the Sevensleeper.
"I have to ask you something.
Am I or am I not a sevensleeper?"
"Of course you are," said his father.
"Then it isn't right
that I have only one brother.

A real sevensleeper
has seven brothers."
"Well, what are we going to do?"
said his father, who didn't know
where he was ever going to find
so many brothers in such a short time.
"Just one new brother
takes a pretty long time," he said.
"No," said the Sevensleeper,
"I need them now."
"Well," his father consoled him,
"you already have one."
"He's useless,"
said the Sevensleeper.
"I need seven brand-new brothers.
Better ones. And right away.
Septuplets."
"Impossible," said his father.

"If it's impossible,"
said the Sevensleeper,
"can't you at least take
my little brother back?"

"Do you know
what today is?"
asked his mother.
"Wednesday,"
said the Sevensleeper.
"Yes, and?"
asked his mother.
"A rainy day,"
said the Sevensleeper.
"Yes, and?"
asked his mother.
"That's all," said the Sevensleeper.
"Today is Sevensleeper Day,"
said his mother.
"Really?" said the Sevensleeper.
"I didn't know that."
"Once a year
there's a Sevensleeper Day,"
said his mother.
"And for seven weeks
the weather will stay
just the way it is today."
"Really?" said the Sevensleeper.

"Yes," said his mother.
"But it's raining," said the Sevensleeper.
His mother nodded.
"It doesn't matter,"
said the Sevensleeper.
"As far as I'm concerned it can rain
for seven weeks.
As long as it's Sevensleeper Day."

 "Time
for bed,"
said his mother.
"No,"
said the Sevensleeper.
"And why not?"
asked his mother.
The Sevensleeper put on his jacket.
He said, "Because now I have to go
into the woods and look for food."
"Couldn't you please do that tomorrow?"
asked his mother.
"Am I or am I not a sevensleeper?"
said the Sevensleeper.
"Of course you're a sevensleeper,"
said his mother.
"Then I have to go
into the woods at night,
but I promise
I'll be back
in time for
breakfast."

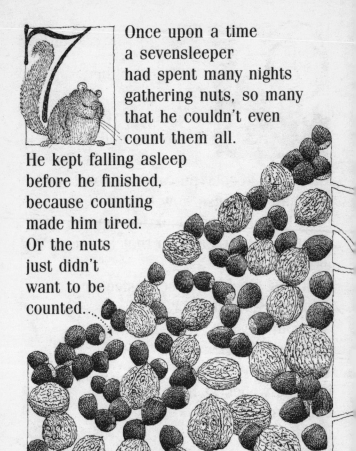

Once upon a time
a sevensleeper
had spent many nights
gathering nuts, so many
that he couldn't even
count them all.
He kept falling asleep
before he finished,
because counting
made him tired.
Or the nuts
just didn't
want to be
counted....

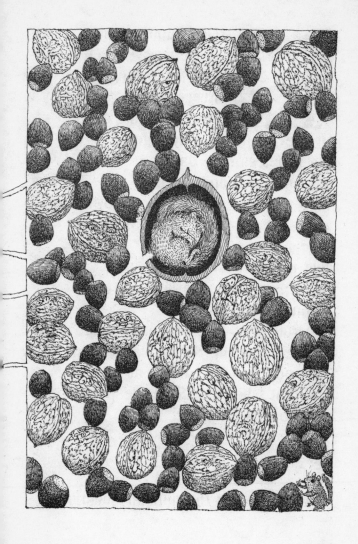

 Once upon a time
there was a sevensleeper
who had seven friends.
Every day he could play
with someone else.
Or they could all play together.
Nevertheless, one day
none of his friends had any time for him.
"You can play with the new boy
who lives upstairs," said his father.
"The new boy is dumb,"
said the Sevensleeper.
But he rang the doorbell upstairs
and asked,
"Do you want to go roller-skating?"
That evening the Sevensleeper said,
"The new boy isn't dumb at all."
And that's how the Sevensleeper
made a new friend.

And now comes the difficult question:

Will the Sevensleeper
have to pick a fight
with one of his old friends?
Or can a sevensleeper
have eight friends?

Once upon a time
a sevensleeper
counted his teeth
with his tongue.
And he discovered
that he had too many.
That made him very sad.
A real sevensleeper
has exactly seven teeth and no more.
He had already lost
his first two teeth,
so there were certain words
such as *sausages* and *Mississippi*
he couldn't pronounce right anymore.
But he still had
too many teeth.
He tried to figure out a way
to get rid of them.
"The dentist
can pull some of your teeth,"
said his brother.
"You nitwit," said the Sevensleeper.
"They can fall out on their own."

His tongue was always
on the look-out for loose teeth.
After all, what's a sevensleeper
to do with twenty-two teeth?
But luckily,
two of them started to wiggle.

September 15th
September 27th

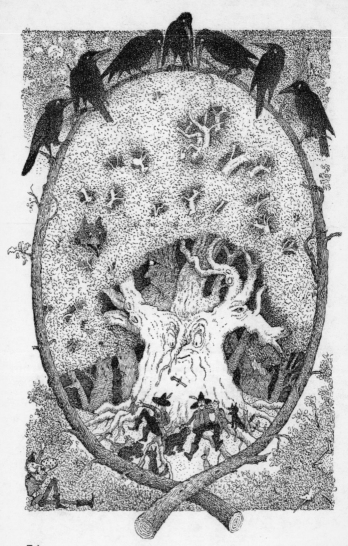

Once upon a time
a sevensleeper
learned to read.
He lay on the carpet
and leafed through
an old storybook.
His favourite stories were
"The Seven Ravens,"
"Snow White and the Seven Dwarfs,"
and, of course,
"The Brave Little Tailor,"
who always got seven in one blow.
He used to like the one about the six
who travelled all over the world,
but now there was one too few.
And what was he supposed to do about
one of his longtime favourites,
"The Three Little Pigs"?
It was really a pity.

"I have seven fathers,"
said the Sevensleeper.
"One for every day
of the week.
All week long
they look forward
to being with me.
Then they want to
play with me
and forget about their work.
And that's not so bad.
But it can get to be a bit too much.
Sometimes I just need
a few minutes by myself.
And I need a good deal of time
for my seven friends.
My fathers don't always understand
that because they see me so rarely.
Then I have to tell them,
'You can play awhile
with my little brother.
You'll see, he's all right
once you get used to him.' "

Naturally,
the Sevensleeper
also had seven mothers.
Every morning a new
mother ruffled his hair.
His Monday mother
had forgotten
what he had promised
her last Monday.
When she thought
he should put away
his toys,
he said,
"I'll do it tomorrow."
That was all right with her.
So his Tuesday mother had to deal with
putting the toys away.
And his Tuesday mother was happy
to pass along the responsibility
to the Wednesday mother.
So they were all satisfied.
They were all different.
Except for one thing:

"They all like me better
than my brother."

 What happens
on a sevensleeper's
birthday?
He turns eight.
And then?
What will happen
to him next year?
The Sevensleeper thought and thought
but he couldn't think of an animal.
No matter whom he asked,
no one had an answer.
"It doesn't matter.
Either I'll become an eightsleeper
or I'll just have to start counting
again from the beginning."

 The Sevensleeper
opened his diary
and read everything
that he'd already
written.
"I didn't know," he said,
that so much has happened."
Then he wrote,
Nothing happened today.
He shut the diary,
hid the golden key,
and closed his sevensleeper eyes.
Suddenly he started to laugh.
"Oh," he said,
"I forgot the most important thing."
He opened his diary again
and drew:

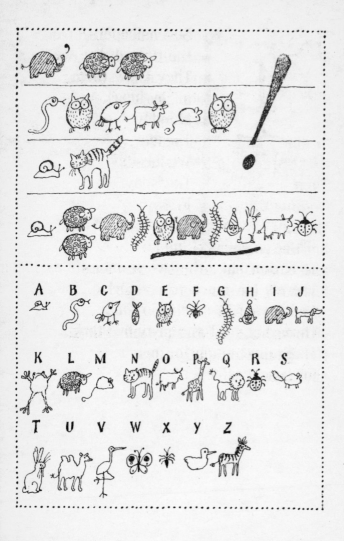

Sevensleepers love
the days of the week.
They know them
all by heart.
Monday.
Tuesday.
Wednesday.
Thursday.
Friday.
Saturday.
Sunday.
They don't like the twelve months as much.
There's too much to memorize.
And a year is much too long.
Three hundred and sixty-five days.
That's just much too much
for a sevensleeper.

 "So what are you
learning in school?"
asked his father.
"Everything," said the Sevensleeper.
"Hard to believe," said his father,
who once had gone to
school himself.
"Not all at the same time, of course,"
said the Sevensleeper.
"What about arithmetic," asked his father.
"Of course," said the Sevensleeper.
"Well then, tell me,
how much is eight plus nine?"
"I don't know,"
said the Sevensleeper.
"I thought you were already adding,"
said his father.
"Yes, but not like that."
"Well then, how?" asked his father.
"We always count to seven.
Then we start over again
and just keep track of the sevens."

"Really?" asked his father.
"Really," said the Sevensleeper.
His father didn't quite believe it.
"That must be a real sevensleeper school,"
he said.

**3** "It's impossible
to sleep in this room,"
said the Sevensleeper.
"It's full of ghosts.
Can't you hear them whispering?"
His mother didn't hear any whispering.
"It's only the water in the pipes
gurgling."
"That's what you think,"
said the Sevensleeper.
"I know they're ghosts.
And they're whispering."
"What are they whispering?"
" 'He was lucky last night,
but today we'll get him for sure.' "
"How dreadful,"
said his mother.
"Exactly," said the Sevensleeper.
His mother turned on the light.
"Now let's see whether
we can't catch those ghosts."
"Of course we can't,"
said the Sevensleeper.

"They only come out in the dark."
"Where are they?" his mother asked.
"One's standing behind the door.
That's the wolf.
One's crouched next to the bureau.
That's the robber.
One's lying on the bookcase.
That's the white rabbit.
One's stuck to the ceiling.
That's the black widow.
One's coiled under the bed.
That's the rattlesnake,
except he doesn't rattle.
And there's one sitting outside
on the hamper who wants to come in.
That's the shark."
His mother shook her head
over so many ghosts.
"Is that all?" she asked.
"Yes," said the Sevensleeper.
"But I think that's enough.
One ghost is already one too many."
"Yes," said his mother. "Or no.

Maybe there aren't too many.
Maybe there aren't enough."
"Hurray!" shouted the Sevensleeper.
Of course, a sevensleeper's room
with six ghosts needs
a seventh to make sure they all behave.
The seventh ghost is the most dreadful,
and the most beautiful and difficult.
You have to figure out a way
to get him first
so everything will be quiet again.
But it isn't easy.
Not many succeed.
And if you do catch him,
he's hard to hold onto.
He has to be treated very well,
or he'll leave,
and all the spookiness starts up again.
The Sevensleeper said,
"The good ghoulie-ghost is missing."
"What should we do?" asked his mother.
"The ghoulie-ghost loves pickles,"
said the Sevensleeper.

"Who would have guessed," said his mother.
"Every night we'll put
a pickle next to my bed.
Then I'm sure he'll come."
"So am I," said his mother.
And whoever doesn't believe this, is wrong.
The good ghoulie-ghost
came that very night,
ate the sour pickle,
and made the bad ghosts
behave for the first time.
"Did you see the ghoulie-ghost?"
his mother asked, wanting to know
just what he looked like.
"Of course not," said the Sevensleeper.
"He's not as stupid as the others.
No one ever sees him."
Of course, it was necessary
to keep the ghoulie-ghost
in good spirits and feed him each day.
But one pickle every night
isn't asking that much to get rid of
six bad ghosts.

Except then the Sevensleeper
had to sneak to the bathroom
every night before going to bed
to brush his teeth again.
Then his mother, who was still
sitting in the living room, said,
"You might almost think
we had ghosts in the house."
"It's only the water pipes,"
said his father. "Gurgling."

A maths problem
for sevensleepers:
One Easter egg takes seven minutes to boil.
How long does it take seven Easter eggs
to boil?

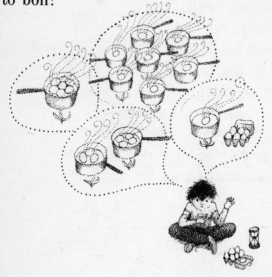

When summer
nears its end
and the days
grow shorter,
a sevensleeper has to
eat an awful awful lot.
Why?
For his hibernation, of course.
He has to grow fat.
You have to be fat,
otherwise you can't sleep.
Candy and lollipops,
cake and chocolate
are best for fattening up.
Deep in the bushes
under his bed
the Sevensleeper keeps a nest.
That's where he collects sweets.
No one else is supposed to know.
"That's mean," said his brother.

One evening
the Sevensleeper said,
"I'm going to tell
you a secret.
Tonight I'm going to
start my hibernation."
"We're really going to miss you,"
said his father.
"It can't be helped," said the Sevensleeper.
His father ruffled his hair.
"You can wake me up again in May,"
said the Sevensleeper.
"What about Christmas?"
asked his father.
"Sevensleepers aren't
interested in Christmas," he said.
"And what about Easter?"
his father asked.
"Sevensleepers aren't
interested in Easter," he said.
"Then I'm sure you're not
interested in your birthday,"
said his father.

"Of course not,"
said the Sevensleeper.
"But you can still wake me
by early April.
On the seventh.
Even if it is a little early."
"April seventh it is," said his father.
"Or maybe seven days sooner,"
said the Sevensleeper.
"So I'll have enough time
to look forward to it."

 Once upon a time
there was a sevensleeper
who had soft fur,
big eyes,
pretty, round ears,
and a thick, bushy tail.
In the autumn, when it got too cold,
he curled up with his tail
over his head,
covered his ears,
and closed his eyes.
Then he slept for seven long months.
October.
November.
December.
January.
February.
March.
April.
"Are you asleep yet?"
asked his mother.
"Yes," said the Sevensleeper.